EPIGRAPH

EPIGRAPH

Gordon Lish

A NOVEL

FOUR WALLS EIGHT WINDOWS
NEW YORK / LONDON

© 1996 GORDON LISH

PUBLISHED IN THE UNITED STATES BY
FOUR WALLS EIGHT WINDOWS
39 WEST 14TH STREET
NEW YORK, N.Y. 10011

U.K. OFFICES:
FOUR WALLS EIGHT WINDOWS/TURNAROUND
27 HORSELL ROAD
LONDON N51 XL
ENGLAND

FIRST PRINTING OCTOBER 1996.

LIBRARY OF CONGRESS CATALOGUING-IN-PUBLICATION DATA:
LISH, GORDON.
EPIGRAPH/GORDON LISH.
P. CM.
ISBN 1-56858-076-2
I. TITLE
PS3562.I74E65   1996
813'.54—DC20   96-19753
CIP

PRINTED IN THE UNITED STATES

TEXT DESIGN BY INK, INC.
10 9 8 7 6 5 4 3 2 1

TO DON DELILLO
AND TO VICTORIA BORUS

Through the mouth
that I fill with words
instead of my mother,
whom I miss
from now on more than ever,
I elaborate that want,
and the aggressivity
that accompanies it,
by saying.

—JULIA KRISTEVA

Yeah, yeah, sure, sure.

—F. W. LISH

EPIGRAPH

Dear Members of the Congregation of Saint Firmus,

Please know that Mrs. Lish succumbed on the eighth day of this month, this in the early evening hours and, as had been her wish, at home. I trust you will each be agreeable to accepting my most earnest thanks for the benison of your abiding concern for Barbara and for myself and, further, for your gift of the mechanism in which my wife was obliged to spend the last of her life. Finally, I beg you to make certain the Mercy Persons you furnished to this household over the course of Mrs. Lish's ordeal have word of my inexpressible gratitude to them. There was not a one of them who did not, at every turn and in every need, give of herself without reserve and with uninterrupted good cheer.

What a wonderful, wonderful lavishness of women! Thank you, thank you.

Yours truly,

Gordon Lish

Dear Members of the Congregation of Saint Eustatius,

You will have doubtless heard of Mrs. Lish's passing. Death came, as was not unanticipated, by her having strangled on her saliva. My purpose is not to enlarge upon the unhappy particulars of the foregoing but to impart to you my incalculable thanks for your dedication to the management of the exorbitant circumstances that confronted me, particularly in the light of my not being a co-religionist of yours. Indeed—and I mean no spite by this—I had in fact taken my case to my own when Barbara was first stricken, but these pious people proved, it seemed to me, not a little indifferent to, and perhaps even somewhat irked by, my frantic importunings. At all events, munificence in due course came to me from yourselves and from certain of your brothers and sisters in Christ, most pertinently the parishioners at Saint Firmus. Bless you all—and thank you one and all for your provision of a crackerjack corps of Mercy Persons. The presence of these selfless creatures at Barbara's side was in every wise a godsend. Will you please hasten to convey to these superb ladies my most heartfelt thanks? One further item—with respect to the machinery acquired for Mrs. Lish when she was no longer able to lie down or to sit, my understanding is that this piece of equipment is to be construed as a permanent installation of this household. I remark this point on account of an unfortunate harshness erupting whilst Mrs. Lish was being taken from the premises—namely, the rebuke I was made to enforce

when someone claiming she was acting on behalf of yourselves sought to remove, with the remains still in place
within it, the device in question. A regrettable misunder-
standing, to be sure, not least because this curious imple-
ment has collected onto itself the whole of the appalling
narrative whose scription was begun seven years ago when
the awful news of Mrs. Lish's affliction was first made
known to our little family of two or three. In brief, there
has, in my heart, arisen, in the parlance, a "sentimental
attachment" to this at once morbid yet life-sustaining appliance. I know I need not, on this point, say more.

Yours gratefully,

Gordon Lish

Dear Clerk of the Court,

I beseech you to realize that Barbara Lish is deceased. Even if she were not and could be, by her nurses, delivered unto you, she would nevertheless make for a less than effectual juror, given that no part of herself, save for her eyes and for her eyelids, had for ages been competent of the merest exertion. May I therefore ask you to desist in sending these notices to this address? They are most bothersome, most exasperating, most inconsiderate, considering. I am confident you will review the matter with all alertness and come promptly to a suitable resolution thereof—namely, the erasure of this figure's name from your files. Let me also state that I might at this time have further recommendations to put before you were it not for my having, by virtue of a piece of the most preposterous inattention, just caused there to happen a mishap of the maddest kind, this when I this morning, prior to my venturing to the front door to gather up the morning's mail, of which your document was the sole particle in this category, came in here in through the kitchen door here after my having visited the night away—or visited away the night—with, if you take my meaning, a certain neighbor lady. At all events, I once again implore you to put an end to this nonsense. It is now several times that your office has directed to my dead wife a summons for jury duty and as many times that I have, in good faith, indicated, by return post, the precise specifications of her physical status. Surely there is in this incorrigible conduct of yours no question of your display of a certain nuance of callousness toward the sensitivities of her surviving spouse, would you not say? Please, no more, I beg you.

Very truly yours,

Gordon Lish

Dear Mrs. Gekker,

May I please say to you thank you to you for all that you did, have done, were doing for Mrs. Lish? You, more than any other Mercy Person who was here at her labors here on these premises here at the time here, are to be cited for an insuperable contribution to my poor Barbara's care. I will always cherish you as the best of the field, there being some among that churlish number whom I found, as I deeply suspect you to yours did also, not at all to my taste, let alone to my liking. Some—we will not be so unkind as to single out, by name, such personages—appeared to me to be little less than roughnecks, if not actually full-fledged criminals, would you not you yourself say? Worse still, I can think of two or three of these hooligans who consistently offered of herself irrefutable evidence of her having not the least experience with, not to mention impromptu insight into, the meaning of the word clean. Yet did it not occur that no complaint of mine, however righteous its purpose and however clamorous its petition, was ever heard above the din of the coarse noise conceived in the fall of those paltry coins flung in my direction in charity? In any event, I somehow sense that you and you alone saw eye to eye with me with regard to so very much that was germane to regulating the decorum of this household during the unholy period when you still graced this dwelling with the very genius of your unparalleled ardors. It is on this account, accordingly, that I deem it entirely proper to say to you that I esteem you, in the context of Mercy Person, as my special and my enduring and my precious friend. Quite honestly, with reference to those who pretended to be your sisters in tenderness, I hope never again to catch sight of a one of those good-for-nothings. A more ruinous batch of slatterns I think I shall never see, nor would, even were I to be in the direst condition of injury, want to. In keeping with this mood, let me remark the grisly fact that there has happened the most wretched of mishaps—yet terrible as is the incidence of this accident, I somehow intuit that there might be in it a detail of the very first importance to me—and it is toward this very end, toward adumbrating the founding terms of that very detail, that I invite you to think along with me for the merest instant. To wit, you will, I daresay, recall with no difficulty the plate on which Mrs. Lish required all the ladies to carry to her her morning and then again her evening suppository of morphine. One could hardly, to be sure, have forgotten how particular this wife of mine was with respect to this requirement of hers, could one? Naturally, in a household quite as fastidious as this one is, much must accost the outsider, if you will pardon this clumsy designation, as having a peculiarly pugnacious bearing. At any rate, do I myself require too much of you when I ask of you that you please inventory the multitude of, let us say, of strangenesses that you witnessed whilst acting as a caretaker for Mrs. Lish, this to determine if you might extract from among such material the exact language it was her practice to invoke when—speaking by instrument of her letterboard—Mrs. Lish struggled to remind all present concerning the identity of that plate? Or of that, if you will—if I am wrong in saying plate—dish? Oh, but you do know the very thing I mean, don't you? Well, enough of this. One in grief, as I am in grief, would do better, I suppose, to coerce one's few remaining energies elsewhere. Still, I should be ever so thankful to you and so irretrievably in your debt for any return word touching however lightly upon this topic. Or phone me if you like. Again, thank you very much for so very much. Not one other of the Mercy Persons was anywhere so worthy of the name. Your colleagues—I intend no insult to you in grouping you with them as such—were, to a woman—to a woman!—as you yourself seemed certainly to have surmised for yourself—filth.

All yours in all good faith,

Gordon Lish

Dear Mrs. Hennessey,

Since it was you and Mrs. Florism who were at Mrs. Lish's side at the last, I am writing to you both for the purpose of, first, thanking you for the exceptional vigilance you were called upon to enact, and, second, to assure myself there is in you and in your comrade not one trace of doubt with regard to my intention to break with custom and come to you to the back with you when I had had my initial indication that a seizure of an extraordinary stubbornness was in prospect of being in progress. I was on the way, dear woman, I was most absolutely on the way. It is my most vehement mission to be assured that you and Mrs. Florism are assured on this point, this in every keen degree—should there happen to be—in your mind, in your mind!—the smallest jot, the smallest tittle, of a thought to the contrary. Too, be informed for the record that I shall presently put before Mrs. Florism the same statement of fact, so utterly unnecessary as my doing so nonetheless is. As a formality, then, in the fulfillment of no more than a formality, I declare that any tint of dubiety be stripped from the canvas, for it has no reasonable place in the picture. Is this errand now completed? May I hope that this errand of mine is now completed? Because, yes, I do freely admit to my having heard the first report of there having produced itself from Barbara a little cough of sorts, yes—and, further, do admit, no less freely, to my very promptly thereafter having come to realize—in my mind, in my mind!—that this note of an incipient turbulence might come to be the preamble to a full-blown episode, and that, in consequence thereof, that Mrs. Florism and yourself might—I am speaking of my emerging realization and of the quality of rumination that accompanied it—might, the two of you, profit from there being, as it were, a further set of hands present to you there in the room with you—for, let us say, for the act of buttressing, should this be needed, the attentions of those predominantly charged with the responsibility of putting into play the usual repertoire of emergency procedures known to all parties constituting the squadron of Mercy Persons. That the ensuant emanation of a jibby-jibby, this not on the floor of the kitchen itself but, rather, along my route back to the back of the house to you, detained me for less than the wink of an eye is true, is true, but it is false—unimpeachably false!—that this fact can in any wise be argued to have asserted itself in the composition of all those otherwise ghastly facts that now give us—and that gave Barbara, that gave Barbara!—the tragic, although not cruel, I would allege, not cruel outcome the evening of the eighth day of this month. For my part, I say, at any rate, let us now be done with all this melancholy and from this moment forth be instead concerned to seek the means of renewing ourselves. Have I told you I am seeing someone? I am, dear woman, seeing someone. Indeed, I am, it felicitously happens for me, seeing not one but two ladies, one who delights in confecting cakes, another who delights in consuming them. Such a piece of luck as this indubitably is seems to me the hand of purest providence having now reached itself into the midst of this mourning of mine to effect a gesture that promises perhaps to preserve me—if only for a while— for a whilst!—longer.

Yours,

Gordon L.

P. S. Imagine this—Louise and Lucilla, these are their names. Do I shame myself in confessing my sometimes, when in their company, confusing that it is Lucilla who is Lucilla and Louise Louise? Oh, but—will you just listen to the fellow boast!—such is the novelty of this bounty that is now so blessedly his.

Dear Mrs. Fez,

What a beacon unto me you were! If the years of Mrs. Lish's languishing may be said to have been a night, then were you not in it as the moon and all the stars? The others, was there a one among them who did not draw the shades over this heart of mine already so in darkness with despair? But all this sorrow, is it not all behind me now? The air I this minute breathe, I must tell you, dearest person, it seems to me so refreshed with its having enjoyed a passage through day. Yes, yes, there have been a pair of dismaying setbacks, I don't deny it—a dish that was broken, a plate—my fault, my fault, my fault, most entirely my fault!—this and the impossible folly of a certain office of our city government inspired to believe it might, by reason of a program of the blithest perseverance pitted against the very rule of nature, that it might rehabilitate Barbara to life in order that she might be pressed into service as a juror on a jury, this latter a modest annoyance at the very precipice, I must tell you, of flourishing into a behemoth of a peeve. But setting these nettlesome matters aside, I am able to make an honest prognosis of the accelerating recovery of my emotional well-being. I sleep well—and although I keep close to home—the sole departure from this pattern being more for the carnal than for the romantic experience—and continue to feel rather more comfortably disposed here in the kitchen than elsewhere in the apartment, I expect it can be claimed that I am coming around and again taking more and more charge of myself. There is, for instance, a certain Louise in my life and, as well, a Lucilla. Barbara is gone and Barbara is grieved for, most perfectly, most perfectly—but each day her ghost seems a trifle more prepared to take up less space in the ether that has been so suffocatingly enshrouding me. Does your life go well? I hope so—and pray so. Speaking of which, not to be surprised if there results in me a decision to undergo conversion to your religion. I will say not one more syllable on this subject, inasmuch as my mind has not, on same, yet made itself up. Do you hear from any of the other Mercy Persons you not so very long ago put your shoulder to the wheel here with whilst so selflessly working your fingers to the bone for Mrs. Lish with? Quite actually, I would imagine you prodigiously fortunate not to have. Apart from yourself, was there a one of them whom I, Gordon—Gordon!—would give you two cents for? Not likely, I can tell you. Scum, this was my perception of the matter—scum and low-life and unsavory specimens of the vilest rabblement. Will you tell me who, who, who was the creature who persisted in discarding onto the floor every crumb of every bran muffin she kept continually importing onto the property? Heaven forfend that this personality turn out to have been the very same bit of dreary goods whose insistence on outfitting herself with rubber gloves and on drinking her tap water only from the disposable cup that she kept sealed away with her in her handbag with her aroused such ire in me. No, no, my good woman, my very Mrs. Fez, let me hurry to withdraw that so impetuous an interrogative—for if you can indeed fetch from memory the identity of this unpardonable slut, I, Gordon—Gordon!—solicit instead your wrapping the news of your knowledge forever in silence. I want none of it, none of it, none of it!—no rememberings, none!—but only to remark aloud how glad a moment it was for me when I came to discover you standing newly at my door, your sleeves already rolled up well up past your elbows in order that you be not one instant delayed in your zeal to pitch in! When I think of it, when I think of it!—of the unendurable care with which you would sit in here with me to inscribe the codes for signifying the liquefying dates and the specifying of the foodstuffs onto the little labels that were used to denote the history and the contents of the containers we had to daily place—for the nutrition of you-know-who, of you-know-who!—into storage in the refrigerator, not to mention very possibly into ditto in the freezer!—or think—think!—how reliably quick a study you showed yourself to have been in so promptly bending yourself to the task of snatching up from the floor the odd jibby-jibby where there was on the floor the odd jibby-jibby to be dealt with—well, when I think, Mrs. Fez, when I, Gordon—Gordon!—think! Ah, God, you are missed, so very sorely missed—and must come to me whenever you wish, should there be reborn in you, as there once so every so often was once born in you, a yen to sit with me in my kitchen with me and to join in with me in the contriving of an artifact of conversation whilst exploiting the sedate pleasures awaiting us in a dish of Social Tea Biscuits. But which is it, may I ask, dish or plate, plate or dish?—that very piece of tableware that Mrs. Lish was so in the habit of demanding her morphine suppositories be brought to her on? It was kept, if you will only bestir yourself to make a mental map of that region of the kitchen where the sterilizer stood, it was kept just next to it—leaning away from it, resting in a sort of slot formed by the edge of that appliance on the one side and, on the other, by that of the adjacent cabinet on the other. Do you see what I mean? Granted, I am encountering some encumbrances in establishing the exact expression of my meaning, but you do take my meaning, don't you? All right, she— Barbara, Barbs—then, Barbs—she called it what? Not plate or dish, I don't mean plate or dish, but as to Roselle or something, something like some sort of Royal Roselle or something—and then something else insofar as its being a thing of porcelain or, however you say it, a thing made out of porcelain. Because she never said semi-porcelain, did she? Via her letterboard, I mean. Well, skip it. Not important, it's not important. What's important—which you, Mrs. Fez, and only you, Mrs. Fez, would be the first to go along with me on—is the billions and billions of jibby-jibbies its shattering—cheese and crackers!—distributed. Or does one say propagated? Unless what's said is—is it?—

made manifest. Well, what's important is which is it, which is it?—uncarpeted or noncarpeted? I know I can count on you. If there is anyone I know I can count on, then I know it is you that I can do it on. Something else—strewn and deign or deign and strewn—yes, of course, yes, of course!—but these, valued confederate, are they not, at this stage, and must they not remain at this stage, an unrelated consideration?

Yours in His Precious Blood,

Gordon L.

P. S. If nonrelated, then nonrelated. Meanwhile, do, I ask you, please to suspend judgment with relation to the question of hyphenation. Ditto nonhyphenation—to the one, ditto, of nonhyphenation.

Dear Clerk of the Court,

Leave me alone. Can't you leave me alone? Be a sport and leave this household be. Have you no respect for the dead? Please, please, this must come to an end.

Very sincerely yours,

Gordon Lish, in desperate grief

P. S. Or is it that it's your dirty vicious rotten scheme for you to see what kind of crime there is for you to cook up and charge me with for opening up her mail? So is this it? Did I guess right? Is it that I, Gordon—Gordon!—just happened to hit upon your filthy game? Because I would not put it past you, you bastardo! And never mind about the commas, okay?

Dear Mrs. Kreshka,

Play a game with me for a minute? As to, you know, as
to just making believe for a minute it's back, we're back to
when Barbs was still with us and you were still coming to
us and you've just come in the door to us and the Mercy
Persons on the nightshift are just getting their things
together and are just going off together and you come into
the kitchen to me and you say hi hi to me and then you go
get the plate and I go get the suppository from the freezer
and then you go with it back with it to Barbs with it and
you say hi hi to Barbs and you put down the plate—okay,
the dish, you put down the dish—you say hi hi to Barbs
and you put down the dish and you go hit the switch to let
the Lauchesset back down a little bit so that it's not so tilted
back so far so much as it was when it was where the other
ladies left it and Barbs sees yikes, sees whoops, sees hold
onto your hat, sees the impeccable Mrs. Kreshka has gone
ahead and, can you believe it, she's come with my suppository on a dish other than on the dish everybody's supposed
to know by now I want my suppository to come to me on.
So what she does is she, so what Barbs does is she gets her
eyelids hiked up heavenward whilst phonating as per,
whilst she phonates AAAAAAAA and then AAAAAAA and
then AAAAAAAA and then EEEEEEEE and then
EEEEEEEE and then EEEEEEE, whilst all the while
widening her eyes and gaping with her eyes to where she's
guessing the letterboard was left when last it was used by

the ladies on the nightshift. So, yes, yes—strikes a chord, does it? Takes you back, does it? You get the letterboard, you get squatted down in front of her with the letterboard in front of her and then Barbs spells what? You remember what? Not that you ever didn't get her the right dish for her—but making believe, can you play the game with me and make believe with me? Barbs spells what first? Spells Roselle something first, does she? Or spells Royal something first? Spells which first, which? Or are you all telling me she never didn't make it a point to spell P-O-R-C-E-L-A-I-N and never S-E-M-I etc. porcelain? Forget it. Ridiculous. I'm ridiculous. Gordon is ridiculous. This is ridiculous. Where's the significance in any of this? There is no significance in any of this. Skip it, skip it, skip it. I keep bothering people. Sorry I keep bothering people.

Your very good friend,

Gordon Lish, widower

Dear St. F,

No, you may not have it back and that's that! Which goes both for you and for your sleazy pals at St. E's, clear? I make myself clear? Or would you like to speak with my attorneys? Because, don't worry, I've got attorneys!

Yours very sincerely,

Lish

P. S. Or "to" my attorneys—if this is what it takes for somebody to make himself understood to you people. Or "by" you. People, I mean.

Dear Mrs. Bosoodi,

Just wondering if you might want to come over here for a little bit and sit yourself down and take a load off and maybe share a plate—a dish—of Social Tea Biscuits with me and then afterwards we could probably pray together, if this was okay with you. Because I have been devoting some very serious thought to the question of if whether I should convert or not and was thinking maybe having some meditation with you could, you know, help me go ahead and make up my mind about it.

Yours in preparation for sanctification,

Gordon L., in transition

Dear St. E's,

Could I explain something to you? I'm going to explain something to you. What's mine is mine. You people never hear of squatters rights? Look it up—squatters rights. I'm sitting on it. I am reclining on it. It's tilted at the three-quarter tilt, which is the best tilt for me to be tilted in it at to write assholes like you letters in it. Anyway, get the fuck off my back!

      Yours in impermanent patience,

      Mr. Gordon Lish

P. S. Maybe it would interest you folks for you to know that I happen to be on a personal basis with the Clerk of the Court. As far as apostrophes go, forget it.

Dear Mrs. H.,

Any advice for me as to how for me to possibly, without hurting her feelings, for me to get her to quit making angel-food cakes for me and maybe for how for me to get her to switch instead to devils-food cakes instead for me—Louise? Because, one, the freezer is chuggy-jam with the shit—because, two, Lucilla's bitching about it's high time for something else or else she's going to have to shit a brick—and, three, because, three, weren't you the fucking cunt who was always constantly coming the fuck into here onto these premises with some kind of fucking bran muffins of yours with you in your fucking handbag with you and with your own fucking personal fucking disposable cup with you and with about four fucking dozen fucking pairs of rubber fucking gloves with you? So I, Gordon—Gordon!—was just, you know, tilted back in the old fucking Lauchesset here lounging here in the old kitchen here just thinking, hey, Gordo, could this cunt be the cunt who's the same fucking cunt who, one, looked like she's probably the fucking expert not only on cake-baking but also on catching things from people who couldn't conceivably be contagious to you even if they stood on their left ear to afflict you with what they had, which my Barbara Barbara Barbara couldn't because could my Barbara Barbara Barbara even stand on even both fucking feet even? Or get down off her toes if you could maybe once got her stood up on them?

Very sincerely yours,

Gordon Lish

P. S. One other thought for your edification—which is that you know perfectly well which floor I am referring to and, further, that that particular section of the floor in this household happens to have been, and still happens to be, the only carpeted section of floor anywhere in sight around here in this household, whereas elsewhere around here in this household there's jibby-jibbies galore, which in the eyes of the law you and you alone are legally responsible for, which continue to be in—in the legally liable sense, in the legally liable sense!—in sight. You stinking fucking rotten bitch. Oh, but far be it from me to get down with you down on your rotten level with you and pick a fight with you just like a dirty stinking rotten dog with you. Oh, you heard me, all right, you good-for-nothing filth! Cheese and crackers, do you make me sick. You and you know what? You and your whole religion, that's what!

Dear Mrs. Florism,

What's so wrong with a man who is fond of Social Tea Biscuits? Is there anything so wrong with a man who is fond of Social Tea Biscuits? Some other things I want to ask you because you're the only one in the whole crowd whose opinion is worth the paper it's written on—one, aside from Social Tea Biscuits, setting aside the question regarding Social Tea Biscuits—or is it your opinion that this question obliterates all else? Have I confused the situation about myself because this question obliterates all else, counting all of the other questions? All right, one thing is true, I can certainly see that one thing is true—less Social Tea Biscuits in the house, less jibby-jibbies in the house. Or does it lower me in your eyes for me not to have said fewer? One way or the other, lower or not, there is always the possibility, remote as it may be, of a nonrelated, or of an unrelated, possibility. If I am wrong, tell me I am wrong. Hesitate not. I could not bear to think that you might be at all hesitant not to hesitate me not. Come see me. I want to see your bosoms. Yours are the bosoms that tremble, not the bosoms that shake. If I am wrong, if I go too far and am wrong, then write it off to the paper I am writing this to you on— but please, please, please, not to breathe a word of this to Mr. Florism for I am very afraid, very afraid, very afraid. Quite honestly, I do not know how I have been summoning the courage for me to "visit" with the so-called Lucilla—as she will not come to me here for us to do it here but makes me come to her there for us to do it there. I am, I must tell you, not at all comfortable "out-of-doors." Another point—the incident involving the dish, it quite plainly would not have evolved into an incident if the so-called Lucilla had deigned to "visit" with me here on these premises and not obliged me to come to her to "visit" with her at hers. Now look at it, now look!—strewn, I tell you, positively strewn. If there is another word for it, if anyone can manage to determine another word for it, then I, Gordon—Gordon!—should like to hear it.

Looking forward to your soonest reply,

Gordon L.

P. S. One other thing—you were or were not in the room in the course of the following incidents?

1] Barbara, or Barb, or Barbs names the canary.
2] Barbara, or Barb, or Barbs names the hermit crab.
3] Gordon—Gordon!—steps into the gishiness.

As for when I was on my way to the back from the kitchen when the unmentionable was happening, I am well acquainted with the fact of your presence there. There was, according to my records, there was your presence there, one, and, two, there was that of a second Mercy Person there. Am I correct in believing this information to be correct? Do my records, such as they are, attest to an accurate, as well as to a reliable, reflection of the correct facts? Thank you. Anyway, come over when you can. I want to see them to see if they really can be said to tremble without fear of contradiction. Many shake. There is nothing wrong with shaking. There is nothing to sneeze at about so far as shaking. But tremble, trembling, this is something to write home about—and let no one tell you—no one!—any different.

Dear Mrs. Florism,

Please, please, please, please—I am so dreadfully sorry for what I said and so unbridledly ashamed of it and am consequently desirous in the veriest extreme of you keeping it to yourself and of you not making any mention of it to your mister.

Yours most apologetically,

Mr. Gordon Lish, in bereavement

P. S. I have, as you might have guessed—and this explains everything, everything!—been under no end of pressure lately as a result of some cocksucker masquerading in the mails as the Clerk of the Court.

Dear Mrs. Florism,

I am really most dreadfully sorry. Don't know what got into me. Something got into me. What got into me? There's no telling what it was which got into me. Anyway, it's spilt milk. Let's forget it. It's spilt milk. The milk's been spilt—as the saying goes. Just don't, I beg you with every fiber of my being, impart one word of this to your mister. Do we understand each other? May I take it that we understand each other? It was you who was with, when with another, with—at the last of it, at the last!—with Mrs. Lish. I owe you everything for this.

Yours in all seriousness,

Gordon Lish, most sincerely beside himself

Dear Mrs. Gekker,

You are the one! God, why is it only now that I know that you are the one? Never you mind! Pay it no mind! There is still time. Listen, I have been dozing lately and dreaming lately. A lot. Yes, yes, yes—what, yes, could be more tedious than the recitation of dreams? I know, I know, I know. But are they not mine—mine!—these dreams? So without further adieu, listen to this. One has a dog in it. It keeps getting bonier in it. Whenever it shows up in the dream, it looks to me to be bonier than the last time it did. This is interesting. In my opinion, this is very interesting. But dispute me if you feel you must. Why I say interesting, however, is because of the fact that the only dog I have ever known about is or are the dogs Mickey and Jack, which were my father Wilhelm's dogs which he kept taking out with us when we went out in the rowboat together for flounder or fluke. Other animals I could mention to you are as follows—Fred the hermit crab, which Barbs, using her letterboard to do it with, named, which event took place prior to, or before, I, Gordon—Gordon!—had undertaken the revisionary tactic of taking myself to the kitchen as a consequence of the notorious gishiness situation. Two was the warbler or the roller or the triller which Mrs. Lish made it her business to insist upon the unfortunate and, as it turned out, unlucky name for—also prior to and so on and so forth. Or have we, dearest creature, neglected to make in the mind—in the mind!—an indelible entry entailing the matter of my coming to restore to order its cage with the Kirby? Now then, did I or did I not get to Lucilla's finches yet? Yet would one were to so do, or have done, one wonders, would not one have thus done, or be doing, by that act that which might incite in you the witchiness you bitches are famous for?

Sorry, got to run now,

Gordon L.

P. S. Oh, but really—if not to you, then to whom? If not to consign the promptings of my

Dear Mrs. Gekker,

I feel pretty impromptu about the fact that I have failed to fill you in on Lucilla and her finches, considering the fact that you have quarried for yourself a place of not unnotable volume in my heart. Let me, then, come directly to the point, then—that I must, namely, turn myself about in display of all myself for it to happen that she, Lucilla, might be able to know whether or not there has come to adhere to my person, this whilst we were, had been, the two of us, "visiting" together, a feather.

Awaiting your thoughts on this,

Mr. Gordon Lish

P. S. It would be smallish and grayish. Or, quoting Lucilla, gray-y. But I am quoting, as I say, Lucilla.

Dear St. E's,

Up yours. I would not join your religion if you paid me. Ask me for it back one more time and be not surprised if swift and decisive legal action ensues swiftly and decisively.

Zay gezunt,

Gordon Jay Lish

Dear Mrs. Gekker,

Did I mention strewn? Or deign? I hate to quote myself. One other question and then I will say ado. Did she ever, when you were within earshot, go UUUUUUU? It goes without saying she might have gone UUUUUUUU when you were not within earshot—and when none of the other Mercy Persons was within it either. Or when nobody was. My God, has anybody given any thought to the question of what if she did it in her sleep and didn't even hear herself do it? But all of the other vowels, don't worry, they are all of them accounted for. Because maybe she did it when I was in the kitchen. I am not saying I was not ever in the kitchen. I was in the kitchen. Except don't think I wasn't, even when in it, within it, earshot.

Yours alertly,

Gordon

P. S. Whose fault is it if everything's strewn? You pick up your pencil, isn't everything instantly strewn?

Dear Mrs. Fez,

Been feeling somewhat off my stride lately. Haven't been lately feeling all that much myself, have I? Feeling sort of out of sorts, I think. This thing of someone passing away, it sort of takes you by surprise, doesn't it? It's probably been taking me by surprise. I don't think I was ready for it. I thought I was all set for it and was all ready for it, but now I can see I wasn't. Actually, I don't think I feel so hot at all. But the idea of what I'm supposed to do about it leaves me sort of really in the dark. It feels like I am really more or less out of ideas of all types—or should I have said as if when I just said it? What was going on was that I was getting out some of the time seeing some neighbors some of the time, but I am not doing it so much anymore. Actually, I was getting out to see only one of them. The other one was coming over here with cake for me. But she's stopped doing it. If I could tell what her reason was, I'd tell you— but I can't. Well, people and their reasons. I mean, what difference does it make if they say they have a reason or if you say they do? Nobody knows. Does a human being even know what it is if it's the reason which, let's just say for argument's sake, the day before it was? But enough of Gordon philosophizing. She just stopped doing it, the neighbor. So what's next on the agenda? That's the philosophy to have. Check with me as to the philosophy to have. But listen to this. You want to hear something she said? She said something which I at the time thought was very funny at the time. It really made me laugh. It really tickled me and made me laugh. It doesn't make me laugh anymore—but this is probably because I am used to it by now and the thrill has worn off of it so it's not so funny anymore. Anyway, it was "Every house needs a cake in the house." I thought I'd tell you so you could enjoy it too. No kidding, it gave me a pretty big kick at the time. "Every house has to have a cake in the house." If I can theorize as to why she probably said it, chances are it was because I was always saying to her, "Louise, is this another cake, are you bringing me another cake, what are you doing always coming over here with all of these cakes, how many cakes can one person eat, do you think I can eat all of these cakes, where did you get the idea that I am such a big cake eater, did somebody tell you I was a big eater of cake, didn't anybody ever tell you I am more of a big Social Tea Biscuit eater than a big eater of cake?" Whereupon her comeback to me just tickled me so. I mean it, it really put me in a good "frame of mind." She said, "A house has to have a cake in it." Well, she should have said a house has to have a ton of cake in it, which is what this one has in it now and I'm serious. I have the whole fridge filled up with it. What's even nuttier is it's all angel-food cake too—or is it angels-food cake? I don't know. Barbs never made any. Her name's Louise. I was taking some slices of them to another neighbor lady whose name is Lucilla. I probably should go ahead and take Lucilla whole cakes to her all at once now instead of just slices. I could take her whole cakes every day and still have plenty of "cake in the house" left for me just for myself in the fridge. But I have stopped going over to see her. It makes me have to go outside to go. I don't like the "outdoors" the way I used to. She had this way she had of getting her heels hooked over around your ankles when you were having a "visit" with her. I was really impressed by it not as a trick but as a way of getting your unmentionables up good and tight together. But I stopped going. Something crazy happened as far as the belt I had on over my coat because it was so cold and the dish I was using to take the slices over with. It was truly crazy. I am still "scratching my head" over it and wracking my brain. Or racking it. Anyway, I haven't even cleaned it up yet, the billions and billions of jibby-jibbies. Isn't this something? I think this is really something. Because you know me, always going crazy getting the jibby-jibbies up. So I suppose I am really changing as a human being, don't you think? All your life you have these ways of yours and then one day you just don't have them anymore. It's the strangest thing. Don't you think it's the strangest thing? It's not because of her passing away, I don't think, but just because I am changing as a human being, I think, and didn't even notice it until enough of the changes piled up. Another thing is it was interesting, the way she would hook her heels around you like that to get everything good and tight like that. Barbs never did anything like that, you know. Barbs did some other things when you were "visiting" with her but not ever anything which I can remember with her heels like that, you know. Actually, I don't remember what Barbs did with her heels. It stands to reason Barbs probably did something with them—but whatever it was that she did with them, I have to tell you the truth, the answer is beyond me. But I don't want you to get the idea that I am sitting here in this thing lounging in it brooding about things like this and thinking what did Barbs do with her heels? Because brooding is not for me. Some people are brooders and some people are non-brooders and that's just the way it is with people. I'm known for having a more forward-looking type of thinking entirely. I always say it's better to look ahead. That's why I was thinking of converting. I'm not thinking about it as much as I was anymore because I think those people are probably just as full of shit as the other people are, but you never know. Anyway, excuse my French. It's just I get pretty hot under the collar when I think about the selfishness of some people, let alone how petty and small-minded they are. But maybe this is because I have not been myself as much as I would like lately. Louise said that her saying about this is "Just make certain the house always has a cake in the house." Well, let me tell you something—I can certainly see the wisdom of this saying. Mind you, Louise did not specifically mean, I don't think, a specific cake. She had in mind just a theory, I think. It was just the theory of supply and demand, don't you think? Anyway, it's not the gist. The gist of it is something else. For instance, I should clean out the fridge and move out of this place. I really probably should. There's no question about the fact that I would first have to go get down and get all of the jibby-jibbies up from when I accidentally wasn't paying any attention and instead went ahead and took off my belt without first getting the dish out of my coat out first. But I don't know. You get one, then what? Look, I don't have to tell you, do I? Mrs. Fez, of all the people in the world, since when are you the one which I would have to answer this question for? If anybody knows what the story with jibby-jibbies is, if it's not me, Gordon—Gordon!—then would it not be you yourself? Anyway, it's the thing about jibby-jibbies. You wet your finger, you push down on this jibby-jibby over here, the very instant you are pushing down on it, guess what's the next thing next! Forget it. It wears you out just to talk about it. How many years was she sick? How many years was there sickness in this house? So with all the traffic in it with all of the Mercy Persons constantly coming and going in it, do you have any idea how many billions and billions of times Gordon—Gordon!—had no choice but to wet a finger and go after this or this jibby-jibby? Plus which, wasn't there one of them which had the gall to always keep coming in here with some kind of a crumbly muffin with her? But do I have to tell you? I don't have to tell you. You yourself saw the whole deal yourself right from the ground up. Which reminds me, weren't you on the job when they came in here with this machine and said it was a gift from them? Because, believe it or not, your brethren have been communicating with me relating to saying they want it back. They say it's theirs and that I was just borrowing it and that they have plans for it and that's that. I'm not talking about just one of these outfits, I'm talking about both. I told them over my dead body. I told them they're not the only ones with plans. I told them I don't have to take their guff and I don't see any reason why you can't go ahead and tell them that for me too if you happen to find yourself in a situation where you are in communication with them personally. You try to explain to these people about things, but they don't listen. I sat here and said to them I'm sitting here right in it right this very minute and possession is nine tenths of the law or nine-tenths of it. You would think these people would have heard about "sentimental attachments," wouldn't you? But no, it's like talking to somebody who was born yesterday. I sometimes sit here and think to myself did these people just get off the boat? Because they act like it. I'm sorry, there's something that's happening when a thing like this happens. I don't know what it is and I wish I could tell you what it is but, believe me, something is. Frankly, I would like to think it's not my religion. Because it's crossed my mind— my mind!—you know. Don't kid yourself, a lot of people hate you when you're my religion. I know it doesn't go for present company, Mrs. Fez, but you can see how the theory probably holds water if you set aside present company. All right, maybe I should have kept this theory to myself—but you know the forthcoming type of a person I am, don't you? My philosophy is it's the best policy to be forthcoming with people, whatever their religion is. On the other hand, I am not saying I have gone ahead with a policy of being forthcoming with Lucilla as to my true feelings deep down as to her setup with the finches. I'm serious. She's got more finches in her place than the jungle has, plus she lets them have the run of the place like they owned it or something. You think I'm kidding, but I am not kidding. It was really something for you to be "visiting" with her there with these finches all over the place in the room with you coming and going with you just as they pleased. Especially since you haven't anything on and they have feathers and little tiny scritchy feet and wings. It's not the reason I stopped going over there to "visit" with her, but I would not call you a liar if you came to the conclusion it was a contributing factor. But there's also another aspect to it too—"visiting" with somebody to beat the band with them whilst there's billions and billions of finches flying their heads off from one end of the room to the other of it with their wings. I bet it's why I always thought to myself devils-food cake when I had Lucilla in mind—in mind!—for a cake change. But who knows why you really have something in mind? She just leaves it open, this little tiny door of the cage. So when you are "visiting" with her, couldn't a finch come and land on you? It could, couldn't it? I'm not joking—I'm serious. Did you ever in all of your born days ever before come across anything along these lines? Because I didn't. Who knows what a bird is thinking? It could make up its mind—its mind!—to just come and land on you for no other reason than it just made up its mind to—and would you be ready for it? No, you wouldn't be ready for it, would you? Well, it's the reason I used to lie there thinking to myself maybe I should make her get on the top of me and have me be on the bottom of her instead of myself on the top of her so that if, God forbid, a finch decides it wants to suddenly land on us, it comes and does it on her back and not instead on the back of a certain somebody who wasn't ready for it. But when I took it into perspective what she did with her heels weighed against the question of a finch landing on you and there's nothing to keep you from feeling its little feet on you, I went ahead and made up my mind—my mind!—to take a chance. Because go figure it out for yourself—she can only do that with her heels like that only when she is on her back like that. I don't think Barbs ever did anything ever anything like that. I'm sitting here racking or wracking my brain about it, but I'm sorry, I can't think of one thing Barbs ever did that was. Unless it's I don't remember it anymore and there was plenty galore back from when we first got busy "visiting" with each other. As far as Louise, I don't know if she does anything at all because we didn't have any "visits" when she was still coming over here with cake for me. Or is it Lucilla? Well, the kitchen's not the right place for it, is it? Whereas in the back, I still don't go back there, you know. I mean it. I know it's nutty not for me not to use any of the household back there, but don't forget, I'm, one, I'm the one who stepped in the gishiness, one, and, two, there's everything still back there except the Lauches-set itself, which is guess where, right? But all those tanks and things, the lines and surge routers and spillways and so on, the hoses and the intakes and the basins and the canulas and the lifters and the flow cocks and the skimmer spoons and the solids tray and so on, that's, all of that's all still all back there in the back of the household back there and I am just not in any type of a position with my mind as of now for me to go ahead and go tear it all out, you know? Look, I am just glad when they came and took her out, they got the Lauchesset hauled up here to the front for me—because I have to be honest with you, it has been making all the difference for me. I generally keep it tilted at about a three-quarter tilt, which is for comfort, one, and, two, for ease with getting these letters out to various differ-ent correspondents of mine on a timely basis. I'm on the job, you might say. Also, the letterboard couldn't make for a more ideal writing board for me to lay the paper on and to go to work. And don't kid yourself, just sitting at a tilt, I promise you, it takes a "frame of mind," I'm sorry, it takes a "frame of mind." Besides, there's the cakes, making room for the cakes, adjusting the location of the cakes—then there's the suppositories which were left over—third, there's the food bags we were always making up for her with your wonderful wonderful various different labels on them. Hey, I've still got about a billion billion of them—BF 6/20 and BN 6/21 and BT 6/22 just to give you an example of some of the B ones. Or how about PK 11/5 and PR 9/4? Not that you could ever get much of any of it in her. But wasn't it the thought which counted, true or false? Well, I myself am not any big fan of roasted peppers all made up into a goo either. Or pork. On the other hand, you could go ahead and dump a quart or three of BC into me any old time there ever was! Something else I love is Social Tea Biscuits. I always loved those two things. You know the two things I always loved? Bacon and Social Tea Biscuits. Well, we really gave the old Osterizer a workout, didn't we? I'm telling you, this kitchen of mine was really jumping back in those days. I guess the same goes for the Lauchesset. But, hey, you plug it in and hit the switch and it just hums right along like just like always.

Thanks for listening,

Gordon L., with all his heart

Dear Mrs. Fez,

The fact of it is, I'm not feeling as funny as I felt anymore. It was just the mood I was probably in. I'm not in it
anymore. I still don't feel like going "outdoors" and "visiting" with her. But wouldn't it be nice if Louise would
come over? One thing is I need somebody to help me get
all of these jibby-jibbies from the dish up if there is to be
any action on the idea of moving out of here. Well, bad as
it is from here from the kitchen door out into the hallway,
it's nothing compared with the feathers all over Lucilla's,
not to mention the feed and the little tiny grit they have to
have for them to get their seeds digested. Did I tell you she
used to have me turn around with nothing on me to give
me the once-over before I got my things back on me and
left for home? The other thing was, I couldn't figure how
Lucilla could walk on that filth. Myself, I can tell you, you
never caught me taking off one stitch until I got both feet
up on the bed. Yes, it really would be nice if Louise came
over. I don't mean because of a cake or because of a "visit"
but just because it would be nice to have some company
without going "outdoors" for it. I asked a couple of the
Mercy Persons if they wanted to—but didn't receive any
replies as yet to any of the invitations as of yet. Well, give it
enough time and even the bag of CK 6/26 in the fridge
won't be any good even as even goo anymore. Did I tell
you how many suppositories that there were that were left
over? I'm keeping them in the freezer so as to keep them

good and frozen. It's a shame about the dish. But I think it is an even bigger shame that I had to find out she was calling it what it wasn't, which would have never have happened if there had not been these two biggish pieces which were down there in the mess. The rest was, you know, all of these unreadable jibby-jibbies. Look, could I ask you something? Do you mind if I ask you something? Can they do anything about it to you if you leave out hyphens? In other words, suppose they come and see something of yours—like a letter like this one—and they say to themselves uh-oh, where's the hyphens, we don't see any hyphens, where does this stinking rotten louse get off thinking he's going to get away with no hyphens? More anon. Bound to be more get-up-and-go for me to get going within a little more anon, you know?

Your friend,

Gordon L.

P. S. Get up and go get up and go get up and go. Now come and get me, you dirty filthy rotten bastardos!

Dear Clerk of the Court,

I am informed of your much-vaunted policy concerning hyphens. Yet further concerning these confusions, word has reached me respecting your much-flaunted policy respecting commas. Will you people stop at nothing? You have no shame, do you? Lucky for you I feel so pooped today. But did you never hear the expression tomorrow is another day? It would profit you to regard yourself as now having done so. Fuck you.

Yours faithfully,

Gordon Lish, American citizen

Dear Mrs. Hennessey,

One regrets one's having to make mention of one's having failed utterly, if not entirely, in one's efforts to lay down a firm basis of mutuality with relation to your erstwhile colleague Mrs. Fez, which person appears in every particular to conduct the stewardship of her social commerce in a manner quite carelessly, if not slovenly. Or is it slovenlyly? It sounds to me as if it should be slovenlyly. Does it sound to you as to how it should be slovenlyly? Let me know how it sounds to you as if it should be. I await receipt of yours soonest.

Farewell and ado,

Mr. G. J. Lish

Dear Mrs. H.,

May I refer your attention to Wilhelm? You recall, or may I say will remember, Wilhelm? I refer to the bird Wilhelm. I refer to what was merchandized to me under the terms of its being a warbler, I believe. Or a roller or a triller, I believe. I ask you to consider this event. According to the terms of my memory, there is no little basis for one's coming to believe that it was your good self who was "on duty" when, one, this very bird was first brought onto the premises, and, two, when the very bird achieved its destiny in the bathtub in the bathroom adjoining the room in which my late spouse of late

Dear Mrs. G.,

Can you tell me what that fucking canary was? Number one, was it a warbler or a roller or a triller? Number two, was it just too dumb for words? Because I refer your attention to these facts—I paid for a warbler but have reason to believe was handed a roller or possibly a triller. Granted, we had it in the household here for how long? If it was for two days, then it was for two days—whereas I don't think the thing lasted for even as long as for two days. That's how dumb it was. God, was it dumb! I promise you, I know finches, which you would agree with me are probably geniuses alongside your canary. But this is not my gist. I, a widower, have more important things on my mind—on my mind!—than to sit around and ask people which they think is smarter, your canary or your finch. All right, yes, yes, it happens that the answer is a finch—but this is not, as a widower, my purpose in writing to you at this time in order that I might pose to you certain crucial, if not critical, let alone discriminating, questions. First of all, I myself never heard it make any noise at all in any way that would lead one to say to oneself okay this bird is now engaged in an act of warbling as against one of rolling or of trilling. You see my gist? The fucking bird—and all that my missus might

Dear Members of the Congregation of Saint F's,

Hello. Good to be in touch again. Glad to see you folks are coming to your senses. Good. Fine. Very well, then, in the light of our renewed relations, I seek at this time to put to you a matter of a most critical nature—namely, adjoining, would you say, or would you say adjacent?

Yours in fellowship,

Gordon Lish

P. S. One trusts that you will take proper note of the fact that one has elected to make no remark regarding if whether it would be the better for one not to have cited the utterances under examination in or within the "frame of mind" sponsored by the presence of quotation marks if not by that of commas if not too by the delicatesse of those of, or if not of, well, of F or of F's? Answer that one!

Dear C of the C,

Do you realize, are you yet aware, have you not been sufficiently made to take appropriate note of the fact that we had to first deliquesce every morsel that went into her! Cheese and crackers, wise up!

Yrs,

Lish

P. S. You didn't lose my address, did you?

Dear Mrs. Hennessey,

What a name! I really love your name! In all seriousness, I would take your name over any other name! Okay, so speaking of names, what is your opinion, pray tell, of a certain person's spouse sitting there—or whatever you call it that you could say she used to do in this thing—and saying over and over again I say Wilhelm? Or actually, as you know as well as I know, w-i-l-h-e-l-m. I mean when this is the same name of the person who was probably the most important member to you of your entire family, true or false? So what would you say about this? Or are you one of these chickenshit goys who is always too scared of everything to ever come forward and express—in no uncertain terms, in no uncertain terms!—any like, you know, like opinion?

Your friend,

G. J. L.

Dear Ms. Kreshka,

It will perhaps stimulate a teensy node of interest in you and in your colleagues for the mob of you to come to learn that the event in which a certain bird suffered the extreme penalty of exploiting the notion of life was, in every wise and from every standpoint, an accident. Please see to it that this fact is promulgated among those dignitaries remarked in the foregoing noun of collectivity. Too, it would accomplish no little toward the restoration, if not toward the recrudescence, of the reputation in which I, Gordon— Gordon!—was once beheld were you to receive with due emphasis the not discontinuous detail that this goes ditto for what happened to the fucking hermit crab.

Vivaciously yours,

Mr. G. J. Lish

P. S. Fred.

Dear C of the C,

With your permission, Sir, I set you a certain constella-
tion of stipulations—that the household is uncarpeted in all
its parts save one, it being further stipulated that the word
uncarpeted is to represent a meaning at no remove from the
meaning of the word noncarpeted; that the manner of a
hermit crab's locomotion produces the acoustical simu-
lacrum of toenails clacking upon a hard surface, it being further stipulated that no effect called clacking would occur
except that it had as its origin such a surface; that the owner
of a hermit crab, its master, would, were the creature to be
encouraged to "have a small stroll for itself whilst others
observe the spectacle of its walking," be made alert to this
animal's whereabouts by, one, virtue of a visual experience
intersecting with the thing's being, and/or, two, by reason
of an audible signal issuing from Fred's "feet"—or shall we
say toenails?—then let us be done with it, Sir, and consent
to say toenails!—achieving contact with the surface beneath
him. You follow me, do you? Very well, then—then you
will deduce for me, please, what the fuck you think the deal
would be if the floor wasn't wood because it had this fucking horrible soggyish fucking broadloom on it, one, and,
two, the person for whose amusement, distraction, pissy little relief from the unrelievable—call it what you will, Sir,
call it what you will!—the thing—Fred! Fred!—had been
brought home—at no minor expense, Sir, at no negligible
nor any minor expense, Sir!—were meanwhilst seized by

such a fit of choking on some rogue divot of her unswal-
lowable spittle that all attention in that place was sum-
marily ripped from its earlier focus and instead made over
to   Oh, you sicken me, you sicken me, you and your
magisterial logic!

In His Name,

Lish

P. S. Don't you dare think I'm through with you! Or,
actually, it's probably think me through with you.

Dear St. Eu's,

I am concerned to wonder would you be convinced to form a more affirmative view of me were you to be made somewhat more sensitive to the key conditions contriving my unhappy career in the world. First and foremost, there were the episodes wherein I was stripped of belief in fair play. These were twain in number. Number one, Mother forbids me to have free run of the contents of her button box. Number two, Father Wilhelm refuses to interfere with the neurotic treatment made of me by his dog Jack. In fact, Father Wilhelm's dog Mickey was just as vile to me as Jack was—but I am undertaking every measure to restrict the appearance of my straining to go overboard in my disclosing to you the case for my being, for my having been, for my never in any instance having been anything other than a victim. Should this program deliver you to the sensation that I am downplaying it to the degree of my detriment, then so be it, so be it—symmetry, balance, poise, these affections all being beyond the domain wherein my personality is tethered. Which looks to me like my cue for getting to the dogs. The rowboats were, you see, tethered. A rope, a hawser of a rope, has been threaded through good stout rings riveted to the snoot of each and every rowboat. Father Wilhelm—Evinrude, fishing gear, rainwear, luncheon basket, portable radio, dogs all grouped into position at his station—stands waiting on the dock whilst Dom or Dell comes to untether the rowboat determined—by whomever of them comes—suitable for the uses of the assembled party. I myself, Gordon—Gordon!—constitute the concluding part of this party. I am in short pants. I have in my hands in a box the bait. It's in a box. I can feel it wriggling around in the box. Wait a sec, just wait a sec!—do you know what fasciculations feel like? Didn't anybody ever tell you what fasciculations feel like? Before you people cracked open your hearts and sent your Mrs. Fez, your Mrs. Gekker, your Mrs. Kreshka, your Mrs. Florism, your Mrs. Bosoodi, your Mrs. Hennessey all over to us here, are you telling me nobody gave you the lowdown as to what the word is for probably at the bottom of what you people were sending these persons over to us here for? Skip it. Forget it. What's the sense in talking to you people? It's impossible to talk turkey to you people. Look, let me ask you something. Can I ask you something? I mean, somebody has to come along and look them up, don't they? So how come I, Gordon—Gordon!—always had to be the one to? Cheese and crackers, will it never be any different?

Fed up,

Lish, to the eyeballs

P. S. Fine, fine, swell, swell—say I said doesn't he.

Dear Mrs. G.,

I suppose you know no vacuum-cleaner—at least in my experience, at least in my experience!—generates greater noise than does your Kirby. Now then, was it I, Gordon—Gordon!—who acquired for the household a Kirby? Or was the party who did this, who negotiated this addition to the household, and who would have no other make of vacuum-cleaner other than the one named, be not myself but the other party constituting the total party of my household? Unmentionable child in it, or of it, not notwithstanding, of course.

Soonest reply appreciated,

G. J. L.

P. S. One hopes to convey the understanding of the totality thereof. Of course, this adverts to happier times—namely, too, to times when one could countenance, without fear of contagion—or, just as unthinkably, empathic sensations—the illusion of a totality.

Dear Mrs. K.,

Do you people honestly think it fair that you insinuate yourselves into my home as virtually residents herein, gobbling your bran muffins at will, distributing the detritus therefrom as if it scarcely counted that a person other than any one of you would be compelled—by force of custom, by force of custom!—to come get it up from the floor, whilst all the while ingratiating yourselves, in a scandalous exhibition of advantage-taking, into the good graces of a woman weakened to the point of pointlessness—do you people honestly think that, given the aforementioned circumstances of your relations with myself and my spouse, do you honestly think that you can just turn your back and walk away from a thing like this without so much as even a faretheewell! Because I am outraged to think that you could think such a thing—outraged, outraged! Filth, you filth!

Yours very sincerely,

G. Jay Lish, human being

Dear Congregations,

If you knew my story, if my story was as known to you as the story of your Lord is, you would probably feel a completely different way about me and be more appreciative of my situation as concerns my current status. The same thing goes for this Firmus fellow you're named after. I don't know anything about him, do I? So if he said to me nope you can't have it back, something which in my opinion was more mine than it was his, you think I probably wouldn't have my lawyer write him a letter telling him you either come across or pay the piper? This is human nature. This is all I am trying to get you people to go along with me with—the fact that human nature is human nature. Okay, look what we have already accomplished. Not bad for people just getting started. Now about me—I had the worst life anybody ever had. I'm serious. I'm not joking around. You might sit there and say to yourselves is he kidding? Fine, I see what you're saying. But isn't everything relative? In other words, he was the Lord, whereas what about me? I mean, I am just a human being, you know. So looking at it from this perspective, let's just go over a couple of things for a minute from this perspective for a minute since there's these one or two things which happened to me in my life which I think should prove to people I deserve more than just to be swept away under the carpet and treated like a complete criminal. First, there was the button box. Second, there was Jack always scratching me. Or maybe it was Mickey. Third, there was the time I was there in the room and put my shoe down in the wrong place and where I did it it was all gishy and runny and squushy and horrible. Fourth, there was when they were taking her out of here and somebody said nine'll get you ten what she weighs, it doesn't come to as much as to probably maybe even as much as forty. Five is the goys, the fucking goys. Six is thinking I had caught the whole ocean and being the happiest I have ever been and then him coming along and just yanking on the line just a little bit and getting the hook out from where it was stuck up into the underneath of the dock with it. Seven is the surge routers, the flow cocks, the skimmer spoons. Eight is jibby-jibbies. Nine is Wilhelm not having the brains to just turn around and go walk up to the other end of the tub. Nine is hyphens. Ten is Fred. Eleven is having to have the job of getting the antenna up all of the way up and of not being able to reach up that high to get it up enough. Twelve is having to wear short pants instead of longies. But does Mickey stop and take this into consideration? Or Jack? What about thirteen? Fourteen was catching a little peek at her when they sort of had her so that she was not all of the way up yet up on her toes yet and were either putting something on her or were taking something off her—you couldn't tell which, you couldn't tell which!—but then I saw her go right back up back up onto her toes again before I could hurry up and look somewhere else. Fifteen is the finches, billions and billions of them, wings and scritchy feet, finches. Sixteen and seventeen and eighteen is always getting angel-food cake or angels-food cake and not being able to say to her you bitch, you bitch, quit it, goddamn it, you stinking lousy rotten bitch. Nineteen is the mail which keeps coming to her even when you tell them can't they get it through their heads it was curtains for her so many months ago it's not even funny anymore. Twenty and twenty-one and twenty-two is never seeing one of them with her brassiere off and they tremble instead of just shake. Twenty-three is forgetting to first get it out before getting off the belt. Twenty-five is hyphens again and when is it that anybody is going to stop to say to themselves he deserves a medal for it, hyphens? Twenty-six is the worms wriggling around so much inside of the box so much it feels like the box in your hands is a heart. Twenty-seven is strewn. Or deign. Okay, that's all I can think of. So big deal, so it came to more than one or two. So I lied—so go report me to the Clerk of the Court! You bastards, you bastardos!—I—I, Gordon—Gordon!—I am not scared of you!

Double-daringly,

GJL

p. s. Suppose I said deign again—doesn't it make it twenty-seven again? Or did I miss counting something again? Miscount again. Mis

Dear Mrs B.,

If you could just see your way clear to coming over here for a little while and spending a little time with me. I just want to look at you again and see you walk around with your bosoms again and hear again you hum to yourself. I never saw anyone whose bosoms looked better when she walked around when she hummed to herself. Unless it was her herself. But you know the story as far as this goes. Number one, she had to stop walking. Number two, going AAAAAAAA and going EEEEEEE and so on and so forth is not what I mean when I say hum anymore. In the dream I keep having of her she screams. Except it is not the type of screaming you would think of as to screaming. It is a different type of screaming. I have never heard this type of screaming. But it is not scary screaming. Or scared screaming. Well, she should be scared, what the man is doing to her should make her scared, but it does not look like it makes her scared. It looks like she likes it so much that nothing anybody ever did to her did she ever like so much. This is why she screams. This is why in the dream she screams. You ought to see it, his whatsis up inside of her unmentionable. He's got straps on it and rings on it and rubber bands on it and buckles and spangles and beads on it. It is the biggest whatsis I ever saw or even imagined there was. It is more like a tremendous dead filthy dirty fish with dust all over it than it is like an actual whatsis of a man. Plus these things make it gleam like there is wet all over it and like it is all held together by these rubber bands which have got like spools of dust stuck up under them and are hanging off of it. Did you ever see in back of the refrigerator? You know when they come and have to move the refrigerator and you see it in the back of it? You know how there is this type of a dust on the back of it? It's like spools and spools of it, isn't it? It's the type of a dust I mean. The dust on his whatsis looks to me just like this to me in the dream. You would think it would come off from how it keeps going along with his whatsis up in her when his whatsis goes all of the way up inside of her. But then when it comes out again, then when his whatsis comes back down out of her unmentionable again, the dust on it is still there, the dust on it is still there on it, there are still these spools and spools of it on it there, plus the fact that it's wet-looking and so tough-looking sort of, like a type of rubbery dust which grows off from a fish. She is meanwhile screaming from it and screaming from it every time it goes up all of the way up inside of her up inside of her unmentionable even though it looks to you when you're watching, it looks to you like how can it possibly, it looks to you like it can't even possibly, like look out, look out, somebody is going to get choked to death from this, it is going to get up so high up inside of her that it is going to choke her to death from this. But is she scared of not even the possibility of this? She is not scared of any of all of this. She is not the one—it's not her, it's not her!—it's him who is the one who keeps getting scared it's getting out-of-hand for him, like this is the idea of it, like the whole idea of this is to keep making it get more and more out-of-hand for him—until it gets so wild-looking nobody can even believe it in a dream anymore, until it's so loud-looking and big-looking where's the room in it for anybody to hear anything or be anything but it anymore, there's no place left for anything else anymore, for even the dog anymore—the dog! But you know what the scariest part of it is? Because this part of it is not the scariest part of it. I'm serious. Because there is a part of it which is scarier than any of the parts of it which I already told you so far of it. Because way before, because even before this stupendous whatsis of his he's got stuffed up her up inside of her, even before there is no getting any more of it stuffed up inside of herself anymore because there isn't any more of it left for her to do it to anymore, even before there is positively not any of it left for anybody just to get it stuffed up inside of herself anymore, look at her, just look at her, she's still jumping up and down on it, she's still jumping herself all of the way up and then all of the way back down on it—and listen, listen, she's screaming A A A A A A A, screaming A A A A A A A, screaming A A A A A A A—which is when you see it, which is when you see it, what's the, what the scariest part of it is. Because, no, she's not looking at it. Because she is not looking at him. Because she is just always looking not anywhere. She is just always screaming A A A A A A A, screaming A A A A A A A, screaming E E E E E E E, screaming E E E E E E E, screaming

IIIIIII, screaming IIIIIII, screaming OOOOOOO, screaming OOOOOOO, screaming UUUUUUU, screaming UUUUUUU—but the way she looks, the way she looks, this is the thing of it, this!—because how can anybody be looking off like that, how can somebody be just looking just off to somewhere else like that, when all of this other stuff is going on like this? Unless you think she's looking at the dog. Mrs. B., Mrs. B., you think that it could maybe be that this is what it is—the dog that she's looking at, the dog? I don't know. I should be the one to know because who just made it up in his mind—in his mind!—but no kidding, I never even had a dog. It was Father Wilhelm that did. Plus which, they were always squatting around with these big black tinkerbells of theirs. This dog, you think to yourself, you go ahead and think to yourself hey, how can anything like this even keep standing up like this, so bony, just a bone? Hey, nobody could sit here and say this about you, could they, just a bone? Well, you know, your bosoms and everything. I'm not trying to be fresh or anything, but couldn't I see you naked? I don't see why it would have to be such a big deal. We could just sit here just having together some Social Tea Biscuits together. I've got plenty. Plus there's cake. You wouldn't even have to take your shoes off. It's probably not a good idea for you to try taking your shoes off anyway. Guess how many jibby-jibbies there probably still are still all over here all over the floor. Because you couldn't guess if you tried. Probably billions of billions, so why even try? Look, you could just open up the front and just show me your top. You wouldn't even have to take anything really off even. You could just walk around like everything was completely normal and hum to yourself and nibble some Social Tea Biscuits with me and let me see them when they tremble. You wouldn't have to tell anybody. It wouldn't be against your church. I'm giving some serious consideration to converting to your church anyway. You know, I am a very tragic individual, you know. I do not honestly think that I am in such hot individual shape either. Come on, I wouldn't do anything. We wouldn't have to do anything. It would be like the most normal thing in the world, you walking around with your bosoms and maybe humming a little and myself with my eyes and ears wide open. Listen, I think something happened to me, but I don't know what. She, at least she knew what. With her, they came and told her what. But with me it's worse. I am not comparing myself to your Lord or anything, but there are comparisons, please bear in mind—in mind!—there are these definite legitimate comparisons. They can't just be swept away under the carpet. You can't just say no they're not there, they're under the carpet. You have to take stock of the whole thing. This is the thing—take stock of it! I don't think your mister would mind. I bet he wouldn't even think one thing about it. Besides, you are probably not even actually a wife in the first place. I bet all of you Mercy Persons just say that, just say it's Mrs., say call me missus, just because it cuts down on the junk of you being with them in somebody else's household with them. I wouldn't tell. Why would I tell? Who do I have to tell? The only people left anymore aren't even left anymore—if what you're doing is thinking to yourself what about the neighbor ladies I said are in the picture. Because they are not in it anymore. One of them, the one who used to make cakes for me, since when has she been here anymore? Listen, she doesn't come around over here anymore. Whereas the other one, whereas the one whose place I was going to with the slices and so forth on the dish and so forth, I swear it to you that I have not set one foot in this individual's place of habitation since when there was the so-called catastrophe with the—pardon me, pardon me!—the Roselle Royal semi-porcelain—which by the way, which by the way, was never any Royal Roselle anything, let alone all pure porcelain! Oh, don't think I don't know. I promise you, I know. All of you people can stand there and think to yourself he just got off the boat, but you know what, you know what? Because you would all be making a very big mistake for yourselves if this is what you thought! I'm wise to you. Nobody needs to spell it out for me. I have been around the block, don't you worry. I have seen some things, never you mind. I was not sleeping on the job, I can tell you—I, Gordon—Gordon!—have not been asleep here at this switch here which I happen to have here on this contraption here, I can tell you. The bastards, the bastardos, they take you for an idiot, don't they? Well, let me tell you something, one thing they are doing when they take me for an idiot is they are making a very very big mistake for themselves who they take me for, let me, in all seriousness, tell you. Hold the bait box, put up the antenna, sit there in the middle of the boat and don't you dare move a muscle no matter what happens! Cheese and crackers, did you ever? He should see me now in this. Wouldn't this be something? I mean, imagine it, if he could see me now in this. Or her—if she could. God, talk about what would make them all sit up and take notice. Because it would really make them do it, wouldn't it? Did I tell you I get it set at a three-quarter tilt when I get ready to get down to business and get a letter written? All it is is hitting the switch, working the buttons. Call me a widower, but don't worry, paper, pencil, letterboard to lean the pencil down on—you never saw anybody with more work on his hands! How many years has it been since she went? Hey, hasn't it been ages since she went? You probably aren't such a young thing yourself anymore. But I wouldn't care. It would still be so wonderful for me to see them. And hum, for me to hear you hum. You could bring me stamps and envelopes and I could pay you back. Wear your uniform, okay? I loved it when you ladies wore your uniforms. Remember Mrs. Kreshka? Remember Mrs. Hennessey? Remember the other ones—the one with the name which was almost as beautiful as your name is—Florism, Mrs. Florism!—her and

Mrs. G., Mrs. Gekker—and wasn't there somebody else? I get the feeling we are leaving somebody out, that there was somebody we are not putting our heads together and thinking of, somebody we are not stopping and counting, somebody else. Oh, will you look at this! Isn't this something? My God, it is really something, isn't it—because I am sitting here thinking to myself Gordon—Gordon!—who is it the two of you, who is it Mrs. Bosoodi and you are not counting when you count up all of the various different Mercy Persons and all of the time it's guess who! It's her. It's you. It is Mrs. Bosoodi herself. The tricks the mind—the mind!—will play on you, let alone the floor. I mean, go ahead and ask yourself how many tricks there are when you have billions of billions of them just to begin with. Well, what can anybody but the philosophers say? These things, they are for the philosophers—and I say thank God this is who they are for. Myself, I just want to see your tits. I wouldn't ask for one thing more if I could just get to once just see just once your tits.

Yours truly,

Gordon Lish

P. S. Mrs. Fez, Mrs. Fez! Will you look at this? Will you just look at it! I mean, there it goes again, just like the floor again—another goldarned

Dear St. Eu's,

First of all, what are we talking about with him, anyway? What do you want to bet me I suffered more and am still this minute suffering more than he ever even dreamed of, okay? Cheese and crackers, you people make me sick with your constantly getting everything wrong! You think you are not causing me agonies everlasting with your constant fucking constant whining about what you people claim your claim is? Like fuck it's your property! Who's tilted back in it right this minute in it? So it's true, then, it's true!—forty pounds of someone is being hauled off out of here out of this household here and all you people can meanwhile think of is gimme it back gimme it back! Cheese and crackers! It is criminal what I, Gordon—Gordon!—have to sit here tilted back and put up with. You know something? Can I tell you something? Fuck you!

　　Yours truly,

　　Lish the Fish

To you parishioners over there at Saint F's etc.,

As if I didn't know. I knew. There's a little shelf under there. There's a shelf for it under there. That's why she made the skirt for it. That's why she went out of her way to make the skirt for it. So I wouldn't see it where it was, the button box, the buttons. Fuck it, playing with them. I didn't have to play with them. It didn't kill me not playing with them. Do you see me dead from not playing with them? Big deal. That's what's wrong with these people, always making such a big deal out of everything! People should just take it easy more. People should just try to learn to relax more and take it easy more. You know what? Can I tell you what? Everybody would be a lot better off. I'm serious. The human race would be a lot better off if everybody just got together and did their best to relax a little bit more and to sit back and try to do their best to take it easy and not get so excited about everything anymore. Look at me and my jibby-jibbies. Thank God I have changed my ways about my jibby-jibbies. You know what I say? I say thank God that I, Gordon—Gordon!—have changed my ways about my jibby-jibbies. If there's anything I can say about myself as far as all of these years since they came and got her out of there back there and then hauled her out of here, it's this—I am definitely definitely changing. I say thank God for it. I say praise the Lord for it. I say O Jesus, Jesus, save me!

Yours truly,

Gordon

Dearest Fellow,

It concerns me to wonder why it is I no longer hear from your office with respect to its now-historic disability in the matter governing the performance of its mind—its mind! Don't tell me there has at last been a correction entered into your lists of citizens available to the city as stewards of its rules. Can it possibly be that you have caused there to occur a deletion with respect to the evidentiary materiality of one who has had no choice but to give up the ghost? She choked. She choked. She choked. She choked. Anyway, what gives, anyway—you giving up on me or something? I am still, for your information, at the same address. Yes, there was a time when I was giving the odd thought to pulling up stakes, as they say, to kicking over the traces, as they say—but then I came to my senses and I said to myself Gordon—Gordon! Well, I am just sharing with you the quality of my thinking. But meanwhilst, I miss you and your summonses and your questionnaires on the other side on the back. So don't be a stranger, okay? I looked at your name on the last one you sent me and guess what. I bet we're the same religion. You like Social Tea Biscuits? What about cake? What type of a name do you think Bosoodi is—or Florism? Fez I figure isn't our religion either, is it?—but, hey, with Gekker and Kreshka and Hennessey, what's the use anymore, okay? Look, if you've got a sec, I've got some other questions for you. Here's the list. 1] Say suction her out or say suction her out, which would you pick? 2] Which is it, outdoors or out of doors or out-doors or out-of-doors? 3] You call it bird feed or bird seed? 4] Is there a record somewhere which tells the Kirby people how many households in this city have a Kirby in it? 5] What's this thing between a plate and a dish? 6] As far as your experience goes, to warble is to what? 7] If somebody says noncarpeted, does that necessarily make them, in your juridical judgment, an idiot? 8] What would you say would be the worst one for you to have to hear somebody come say to you—outtake hose or uptake hose or intake hose or the same idea with only instead with the word basin instead? 9] What was the story as to this goy named Firmus?—plus another one, Eustatius. 10] You any idea what edible FW could maybe stand for? Or here's another one which has got me stumped—FW. 11] I used to know a person who said gray-y, or do you think I am making this up? 12] Where do you stand on hyphens? 13] Did you ever see a whatsis which looked like a fish? 14] Which is worse? 15] What do you think of a bird which didn't turn around and walk the other way but just stood instead with the water up to his ankles and then with the water up to his waist and then with the water up to his neck and then with it all of the way up over his head? So what would you think? Would you think a bird like this was a bird which had some sort of a secret type of knowledge in it which it was keeping to itself and was probably making the right decision just to stand there and see what happens to it if it just stands there and doesn't go the other way? 16] What would you do if somebody said to you for you to do something and you weren't really actually yet big enough yet for you to actually yet do it? 16] What would you do if there was a dog which kept coming over to you and kept scratching your knee for you to know that what he wants from you is for you to scratch his head for him and so fine, fine, you scratch it for him and you scratch it for him and your arm gets so tired from you scratching his head for him that then when you quit it, that then when you can't keep scratching it, that then when your arm is getting ready to fall off of you from scratching it for him and from scratching it for him and so you don't anymore, so you don't do it anymore, so you just can't anymore than you have anymore, but then the dog, the dog, the bastardo, the bastardo, he just goes back to scratching your knee for you again, he picks up his big toenaily big foot again and scratches your knee with it again for him to try to get you to get back to scratching his head for him again—and it bleeds, it bleeds, your knee, your knee! Whilst mean- whilst—meanwhilst!—does anybody even say to you, does anybody even stop and say to you it's okay, it's okay, go ahead, Gordon, go ahead and go sit somewhere else in the boat, Gordon? So my question to you is, so what my ques- tion to you is is how come I don't ever hear from you any- more with respect to anything anymore? I don't know. Talk about betwixt and between. Could I even get a line in to see if I could get anything on it even? Whereas him, all he ever does is just sit there at the back of the thing with his Evinrude—no, Johnson, Johnson, he called it a Johnson! Yeah, and don't tell me you don't know what Johnson means, you dirty fucking Hebe!

Yours truly,

A patriot

P. S. Is it your opinion I picked the right name when I picked Louise to go with Lucilla? How about Barbara? In other words, Barbs or Barb, which one? Or do you think I should have racked my brain a little more to begin with? Or is it wracked it?

Dear Clerk of the Court,

I come to you with hat in hand. Please, please—tell me if to your mind—your mind!—there is any basis for an action arguing, if you will, or alleging, if you will, whether or not if you were sold something which was supposed to, that was supposed to trill or to roll or to warble and didn't? Or do you think one's opponent in the matter—the defendant, the defendant!—could counter with the claim prove it, prove it? In other words, how can you prove anything if you don't know what a warble sounds to you like, let alone a roll or a trill? In other words, maybe the thing which was supposed to be doing it did it and you, because you didn't know, didn't know! On the other hand, I say praise the Lord. Be ashamed, be ashamed! Do you have any idea, any idea at all, of the magnitude, of the immensity of

Dear Clerk of the Court,

Heaven forbid you should be given to believe I am untutored with regard to the proprieties incumbent upon those who occupy the exalted rank of your   Look, don't think I don't know you're not allowed to give anybody legal advice. I am keenly—keenly!—acutely!—sensitive to the   Yes, quite so, no argument, the question at hand treats a criminal, not a civil—well, question. But you be the judge. I place the question entirely in your hands. I'm sorry, but I am placing it in your hands entirely. Not to mention the fact that the man just comes sauntering over—sauntering!—bends down, kneels down, and gives it this little tiny tug. Whereas I am bleeding. Whereas my knee is bleeding. Whereas heaven above is my witness—heaven! All right, all right—call the police, get the magistrate. I need longies. Where are my longies?

   Yours truly,

P. S. Any chance you could maybe possibly put me on notice as to what type of a case you would have given to her for her to go give it the old, you know, theoretical once-over?

Dear Fellow Parishioners,

So what I want to know is this—which is it which is smarter, your canary or your finch? Or is it not for us to know? But is this the whole story? I mean, is there something the canary knows? Because maybe there is something the canary knows. Do you think there is something the canary knows?

Yours in mutual co-parishment together,

P. S. Your non-warble, your non-roll, your non-trill not-withstanding. Or nonwarble and so forth.

Dear Mrs. Kreshka,

Long time no see. Well, it's the way of things. Anyway, reason I'm writing to you is this—did Mrs. Lish ever do anything to give you the impression she knew I had a father named   I mean, do you think she ever knew what it was, my real father's   I mean the real name of my real

Dear Mrs. Kreshka,

Thought I'd drop you a line. Had some time on my
hands and said to myself, "Wouldn't it be

Dear Mrs. Kreshka,

Do you think I'm a bad man? Did I ever do anything you could personally testify to which would   Were you ever a witness to anything which you would   Mrs. Kreshka, am I ever going to ever have the chance to sit down with you and ever have with you a heart-to hyphen

Dear Mrs. K.,

Guess who. Can you guess who? It's your old

Dear Clerk of the Court,

Talk about your coincidences. I was just sitting here writing to a Mercy Person who was on the job here here in my household here for maybe as many as seven, eight years here. You see, my wife—my wife!

Dear Clerk of the Court,

Please believe me, I would undertake every courtesy to keep myself from making a pest of myself, for I wish you to know, Sir, that I am a fellow not without his notions of self-hood, Sir, and, you know, and, well, of dignity, Sir. But let it not be believed of me, Sir, that such a notion deprives me of the full range of human feeling. I mean to say, Sir, that I feel—humanly—in that very specific sense that I mean I am no fish, Sir, no bird, Sir, and am certainly not, not, not some cribbly spidery gishiness in a shell. Ah, you detect my game, Sir, do you not? The little play I just concocted out of this and that. Some chance bit, Sir, confected into a— well, no matter, no matter, it was either Dom or it was Dell. In the distance, at a little distance, up the dock and along the puffy walkway of the boardwalk—the bait shop, Sir, the bait shop!—wherein one prosecuted the procedure by reason of which one was lent, Sir, the use of a craft. Well, Sir, one rented, was rented, a rowboat, was one not? I myself, Sir, a fellow not unlike yourself, Sir, this in the company of his Johnson, Sir. There were dogs. There were dogs. Now then, to continue, then—there was Lucilla, there was Louise. She died, Sir. She choked, Sir. Let us imagine a fasciculation getting out-of-hand. Ah, you see that I hyphenate. Indeed, Sir, so I do, Sir. Meanwhilst, the bird twitches—the water keeps coming up—he puts down his foot and feels it keep going. I think I screamed. A teensy u, Sir. I think.

Yours sincerely, truly,

Dear Mrs. Gekker,

It has been a while now, or maybe awhile now, since Mrs. Lish's passing. It was, I think we all need to acknowledge, or need acknowledge, a more trying event for us than any of us had been willing to acknowledge. But now that so much time has elapsed, now that there has elapsed such an interval of so much time between the time of Barbara's passing and the time of my sitting myself down here to these writing materials of mine here and of saying to myself, "See here, Sir, since it has been such a very long while since you have troubled yourself to send the smallest civility scurrying in the direction of the invincibly good Mrs. Gekker, is it not time, then, Sir, for you to make amends, then?" At all events, I am terrifically glad to be in a position to report to you that I am feeling splendidly renewed and trust same is reliably reportable of yourself. Quite plainly, none of us—if I may dare to speak, or dare speak, for us all—quite plainly there was not a one of us who was quite willing to quite thoroughly reckon with the extent to which Barbara's passing would—when it came as it woulds must come—enact in us a certain sadness in us, a certain sinceness in us—or do I err in speaking as if I might do so for all? Well, there were times of mutuality, times of assent. True, true, it could not be alleged we came to agreement in every instance. One recalls, for instance, the instance when a bird had been brought into the household in order that it provision it with a certain birdness, which creature, as is customary, need be named, had needed to be named. This is true. This is true. Yet I direct your attention to other creatures—the hermit crab, if you will remember, and the child, whom you will not—each instance an event, or each event an instance, of supreme—may I say of invincible, then?—with your permission, I will say invincible, then—accord. True, true, true, true, there exists no evidence in support of either of these allegments, time having effected a further furtherance of itself. Are you well, then? I pray so. And pray that all good things have come to you as they have, of late, been coming to me. Mine was a cheerless childhood, as you know. I won't go into it. It should be enough to say there was a father, a mother, a button box, names, buttons, and let it go at that. As to him, fishing was his game. He kept dogs, the man—and myself in short pants. Great brutes of things, it seemed to me. The tinkerbells on them, my God! There was a boat, a rowboat, save that it was powered, when powered, not by oars but by a very small, a very tiny, a very little motor. It was fastened to the craft—and could be tilted back—or brought, as it were, forward, as it were—this Johnson, I think it was, or this Evinrude, if that. But he perished—anyway, vanished— somewhere on the concourse of the carpet as if destined for naught but to embark with his shell for naught but disappearance. I believe I called out for him—"Evinrude!" I screamed—or if Johnson, then Johnson—then thus: "Johnson!" No, my God—"Fred!" Naught in answer was there ever ever—"Fred, great fellow!"—heard. She, for her part, could do naught better than first AAAAAAAAAAAAA

AAAAAAAAAAAAAAAAAAAAAAAAAAAAAAAAAAAAAAA
AAAAAAAAAAEEEEEEEEEEEEEEEEEEEEEAAAAAAAAA
AAAAAAAAAAAAAAAAAAAAAEEEEEEEEEEEEEEEEEEE
EEEEEEEEEEIIIIIIIIIIIIIIIIIOOOOOOOOOOOOOOOOOOOO

and surely inwardly—then inwardly, Sir!—then u. I have the
letterboard as a writing board here. Call it an attachment of
the type sentimental. My sentiments are quite exciting to me.
These things remain—her bosoms, her cunning subtraction
of herself to a size no bigger than a minute, the teensiest
glimpse of their taking from her something from her, or of
their adding something to her, this whilst they held the
body—the body!—upright. The screaming, Sir, it was unri-
valed, Sir, at least in my experience. "Firmus!" I screamed.
"Eustatius!" I screamed. I screamed. But came you not, Sir—
came you none of you, if indeed there were ever any of
you. Not that you did not come sauntering to me when
you had quite finished with your flushings lest the seawater
confound the machine. Meanwhile, where was there not
leakage? The broadloom was a ruin. Did I step on it when
that was where I stepped, the wreckage of the tiny shell
inaudible under the fall of my shoe? Did I tell you the
gishiness made me shriek? I tell you, the gishiness made me
shriek. Whereas the woman, with all that paraphernalia
stuffed up inside of her, she plunged, yes, did plunge, yes,
but oh the sweet letter of her composure, the feather of it,
the very feather.

Barbs, I send you all my heart,

Your adoring Gordon

P. S. Gekker, you piece of shit, did you honestly think I'd forgotten where you are, what you are, who you are, that you are—and that she, damn you all, isn't?

Gracious Lady,

How glad I am for this time you grant me. I will be quick
about it. You have my word your patience will be no more
taxed by me than is perfect necessity. There was leakage
everywhere. It left its issuance. What ensued was a ruinous
field of fishy substance. Certain ones of us were undaunted.
I, it vexes me to reveal it, was not among that number. Was
this, however, the sign of a certain insufficiency? It was not!
I am merciful! Who among us is more merciful? You call the
giving of cakes merciful? You call the giving of pussy merciful? Mercy is no act. Mercy is M-E-R-C-Y. I say give me your
straps, your rings, your buckles, your spools.

Yours repeatedly,

Gordon Lish

Dear Antagonists,

Be in every wise assured my assigns are prepared to meet you and yours in resolution of whatever action it pleases you to bring. The property in question is mine. No, I revise—there is no question, the property in question is not in question. Your recourse in law little concerns me—for I shall resort to every means to keep what I have. It is all that I have. The supply of Social Tea Biscuits that was mine I spent to the last crumb when my wealth in cold cake was fast mounting to a fortune my refrigerator could no more contain. Then this too went—was pried from it, was prised from it!—the repairman managing the disposal paid all too eccentrically for the strong stomach it was his requirement to marshal to the job. This is what I have now—the device you insist litigation will make yours. Litigate, then. Come crucify. Do it to me at a three-quarter tilt. See what happens when you kikes come pick on a Jew! I meanwhile—meanwhilst!—remain yours in comfort, innocence, and spite.

Jesus Christ II

Dearest dear

    It's okay. I miss you. It's okay. I'm okay. Please be all
right. There is not one instant when my mind is not   Could
I tell you something Evinrude!   John u

        u

Darling Father,

I am all right. Thank you for taking me. My knee is all better. I had a good time. The biggest thrill of all was when I thought I caught

Precious Mother,

I can't forgive anybody. I am not forgiving anybody. I am not going to forgive anybody. There is not one person who does not owe me. I cannot think of one person who does not owe me. This goes for you and for everybody. I'm sorry. I'm just telling you the truth. There is nobody who didn't just be there and be a dirty stinking rotten dirty lousy bastard to me, and I am telling you, I am giving you fair warning, I am giving you plenty of warning, I am going to get you all back, I am going to give it to you good, I am going to make every last dirty rotten lousy stinking filthy bastard of you wish you were nice to me, wish you had been nice to me, wish you had never been anything but nicer and nicer and nicer to me.

With all my love,

Your loving son

P. S. Name me one button it would have killed you for me to look at!

Dear Father,

I forgot something. There was something I left out. It's just to make sure you knew it was all okay with me about the antenna, one, and about, two, about you not ever saying anything and not ever doing anything after you came over and got down and pulled out the hook. I forgive you. I don't hold it against you. There were things on your mind. Your mind was a billion billion miles away. You never would have sat like that with your shoes in the puddle in the boat like that if your mind had not been somewhere else like that probably a billion billion miles like that away. Hey, I'm the same way. I myself am the same way. There never was once when I wasn't the same way. Do you know what? Can I tell you what? I wouldn't have it any other way.

Very truly yours,

GL 2/11

P. S. Isn't it okay to say who were Dom and Dell?

My very Barb,

Why do I keep saying these terrible things? I wish I wasn't saying these terrible things. If I only didn't keep saying these terrible things. Because, no kidding, you wouldn't believe what's been going on here since they came in here and went back out to the back and then came back out with you and then went out the front door with you and took you all away. Myself, I don't come in and out of that door anymore. Isn't it crazy? I guess it's pretty nutsy-crazy. So is it actually possibly the truth—forty pounds? Because I don't actually believe it, I can't get myself to actually believe it— even though this is what I think somebody said when they got you up from off the Lauchesset and got you lifted up onto something else. Well, I am keeping strictly to the kitchen nowadays. I like it in the kitchen nowadays. Something somebody should tell you—I was on the way as fast as I could. Which is the fact that I was on the way as fast as I could. But I admit it, I admit it—there it was and there I was and that's what I did, wet my finger for it and bent down for it. Then here they come, a billion billion more of them one right after the other of them. Her name's Lucilla. She does this thing with her heels. Didn't you do something with something? I can't remember. I don't remember. All the way home, all of the way home, it was so cold. I kept saying to myself, I kept reminding myself all of the way home. Boy oh boy, if I had only had, if only I had had on gloves! Well, thank God at least—what would I have done at least?—I mean, at least I had the belt. She said don't you have any gloves, you came out without any gloves, how can you go around without any gloves? But I said see this, what about this, all I have to do is to stick it down here down inside of here and pull this belt good and tight. Boy oh boy, did I jump. All of the way home I kept thinking to myself don't forget to take it out before you go ahead and take off the belt off. So, anyway, I forgot. Well, talk about jump. Remember when I was always telling you about the way he was always making me put the antenna up and how I couldn't reach it up to the top? It wasn't the truth. I never ever told anybody the truth. Does anybody ever expect anybody to? Name me anybody. Speaking of which, what actually was it, the name we gave that stinking rotten dirty rotten filthy rotten shitbird of ours? Well, good riddance to bad rubbish. Talk about your semi-something! On the other hand, my knee never really actually bled. Meanwhile— meanwhilst!—I'm thinking five-eighths or maybe even take it down to all of the way down to nine-tenths. Hey, guess what I found in the fridge!

All yours,

2/11

P. S. I love you. I probably do anyone.

Dear Mr. Gutmann,

As concerns your questionnaire, know that I have devoted to it, Sir, ample study, Sir, to have arrived at the verdict that its array of interrogatives is not worthy of reply. Let me, then, instead supply you with statements responsive to what you might have wanted to ask of me had you known your search for data was to fall not into Mrs. Lish's but, rather, into my hands. All right, what is a Lauchesset? All right, I give up—what is a Lauchesset?

God bless you, and thanking you in advance,

Gordon Lish

Dear Ladies,

Okay, what do you say we start first with the Kirby first? I put a little bit of water in the tub and hauled it out. I went and got it out from where it was and hauled it on back to the back and then got him out of there and took him in and put him in the tub. It didn't even hardly cover up his toes. What my idea was was this—let him get himself good and clean and maybe get himself going practicing warbling whilst I went and got his cage good and clean and maybe get him feeling more like finally favoring her with a song. Well, where to plug in the plug? You remember, any of you? Do I have to really tell any of you? It was, as far as lines and loops and leaders and leakage, something, was it not? Plus there was blood all down my leg. What a racket when there's an outlet I can actually get something unplugged out of for maybe just a minute and get her all set up and going, the Kirby, the cage. I don't know. It was probably the power to one of the retro download feeds for the drainage station running to the Dieckmann in her chest. Besides, my knee made it hurt so much for me from where the salt water had gotten up into it into me and then had all dried up again with blood. So I was standing when I first felt it feel as if it was pulling back at me. You tell me how somebody's supposed to hear a little water dripping, how when there's worms twitching, how when there's birds twitching, how when there are fasciculations in the earth! It was wild—the noise, the noise!—the beating of her cunt. Oh, yes, no question about it, I said Social Tea Biscuits, did I not? Oh, the unmentionable on her, the unmentionable! And what she did with her heels, with your ankles and with her heels! It was as if the ocean itself, all water, had grabbed it and swallowed the hook. I screamed for him. I couldn't believe it—screaming for him and screaming for him—"Come!" I screamed, "Daddy, please come!" I screamed. I screamed, "I've got it, I've got it, it's the biggest fish!" Whereas she, for her part, said in silence, picked it out on the letterboard—T-A-K-E H-I-M O-U-T P-U-T H-I-M D-O-W-N L-E-T M-E S-E-E H-I-M W-A-L-K. Walk? Would that it would walk and not just squat, go where it would and not just go where I sat, paw laid upon my knee, big black tinkerbells rolling, warbling, trilling in the boat. You most definitely may not she said when I said sit with the lid off of it in my lap and just look inside of it for a little bit. Then she went AAAAAAAA, went AAAAAAAA, went AAAAAAAA—and every attention was turned upon her whilst hers was turned away. I never saw anything go up inside of anybody or come back down out of them looking wetter-looking and wetter-looking. Well, who has to tell you? Do I have to tell you? Rings on it, buckles on it, straps and things, great spangling spools of things, of wings, of scritchy feet. My thoughts were these—let it land on her. Well, the air, I tell you, it was gray. Or was gray-y-looking. She went EEEEEEEE, went EEEEEEEE, went EEEEEEEE, and I said,

"Fine, fine. It's Wilhelm, then. Then it's Wilhelm, then. Just, please, for goodness sake, just please quit doing that." But he just kept standing there at the tub, the motor rushing so around in it so much. Please, you think I don't know I could have made it Gomco instead of Lauchesset? Couldn't you always have made it something else? I heard her go IIIIII, go IIIIII, go IIIIII, and could tell she was probably going to be going all the way to it now to u. I said one peek, I'll just have myself one peek, how much could it hurt anybody if I just went and had myself just one little teensy peek. This was my thinking. I am trying to develop for you the picture of my thinking. Well, no, they don't actually say morphine on them, no. It's some type of a different kind of a word—but I can't get up anymore and go look at the wrappers anymore. Besides, it's one thing for anybody to keep writing, it's another for somebody to even to begin to read. No sinker, there was no sinker!—so it just got picked up and got carried up and then, when it got to the top, it got itself hooked in up under the dock. O let it land on her instead! Dead when I went back to get it back out after getting the Kirby put back away. Unclean. Jungle, jungle, rubbery with undergrowth, weird snarls feeling all thrashy-feeling in your hand when you had to go uncoil them, some novelty plunging with roots where ghastly fluids had got loose onto plastic, gray-y flora of the sickroom, gray-y mulch of the afflicted, gray-y bone of my Barbara, going OOOOOOO, going OOOOOOO, going oooooo, whilst I, Gordon—Gordon!—come. I'm coming, I'm coming, I'm coming! Never had a chance named Wilhelm—sealed him in a freezer bag, buried him in the trash—whereas Fred, he just didn't ever show up after that. Never should have named anything anything. There was a Mrs. Kreshka, a Mrs. Gekker, a Mrs.   My dear Mr. Gutmann, Sir, it falls to me as my duty, Sir, as befits and befalls a citizen, Sir, for me to say to you, Sir, BL 9/8. I await your pleasure in my Lauchesset. I await it.

And remain meanwhilst ado,

Gordon Jay Lish, whilster

P. S. It's important, jibby-jibbies. To keep getting them, every last one of them, it's probably as important as anything. Listen, I can prove it to you, how important getting every singly jibby

Dear St. Firmus,

Thank you so very much for the consideration you have shown me. Not only did you bear with me during the course of Mrs. Lish's passing but, in the troubling period afterward, you proved charitable and forgiving. It is with every humility that I hope to secure from you your continuing patience with my search for a return to spiritual hygiene. In the meanwhile, how lovely for me to feel myself free to be the custodian, however subjectly, of the object most successfully expressive of the presence whose decline into absence was the grave event that brought us all—I in need, you in solicitude—together. For all this, and for surely more benevolence than I am able to encompass even with the genial agency of that boundless pronoun at my elbow helping me, thank you.

Very truly yours,

Gordon Lish

P. S. Here's one for the philosophers. You want to hear one for the philosophers? Here's one for the philosophers.

Dear St. Eustatius,

A billion billion apologies, please, please, please. Whatever made me think you would be willing to give your attention to the contents of my mind, such as they annoyingly are, I cannot say, but I can, most confidently, say thank you. Why I might have imagined you disposed to holding yourself in contemplation of mental acts having no more actuality than sentences quite convinces me of the unwholesome tendencies that have kept me in their grip since Mrs. Lish, God rest her soul, died. That I should have thought myself in some wise implicated in her strangulation by virtue of my having been only momentarily detained along the way in my rush to give assistance to those there on the premises for the business of, along with that of conveying to her other services, along the way on the way, among them rescue—that of rescue!

P. S. Something else I forgot to tell you

Dear St. Eustatius,

They call it, it's called—the wrapper says it's called duragesic or fentanyl. But, hey, a lot you care, strewn instead of
deign. It's why they have to have letterboards, people like
you. Well, I tried. I shrieked my head off for you, didn't I?
Listen, did it never occur to anybody it could have been a
fish which was really was on it? I had a dog. It got sick and
then it got skinny and then it trembled and then it died.
Hey, but couldn't any dumb goy have said hound? Except
for no, no, no, it died.

Anyway, hugs and kisses,

Gordon Lish

P. S. Come to think of it, now that I think of it, maybe it
was, you know, was the boat, was the bottom of—not of
the dock, not the bottom of the dock—but was the bottom of—it was, you know, that it was the wood under the
boat that I caught.

Bloomington
San Francisco
New York

2 August—23 August

My darling Barbara,

Jesus, Jesus, never leave me in peace.

Your Gordie

P. S. Busted your plate, by the way. Your, you know, your dish. Whoops, something else—looks like—looks as if, as if—he's still missing. But so wait a minute, so wait a minute—saunter! Because that's only so far as he had to probably saunter from, only from only the back of the boat.

Dear FW,

Guess you know where to find me, don't you? Concerning kitchen as concerns where, your duragesic or your fentanyl—oh, fuck, morphine, then!—be damned! Then come, then—scritchy little feet, horrible horrible toes.

Tally ho,

Dad

P. S. Unless it's tally-ho. Hey, another one for the philosophers is how come you only go read it when it's all on the floor all in pieces? Or, anyhow, I mean just the bottom of it.

Chicago
2 September—4 September

Inverted into its formalism,
literature sets out on a difficult course,
its quest of the invisible
becoming imperceptible
and progressively antisocial,
nondemonstrative,
and also, by reason of its being
antispectacular,
uninteresting.

—JULIA KRISTEVA

Nice try, Jewboy.

—F. W. LISH

ERRATA:

Transpose pages 84, 88, 98 and 112, 114, 116.
Transpose pages 118 and 273.
Delete closing epigraph
and replace with
epigraph indicated
one further turn onward.

O come back,
my unknown god!
my pain!
my last happiness!

—FRIEDRICH WILHELM NIETZSCHE